williambee

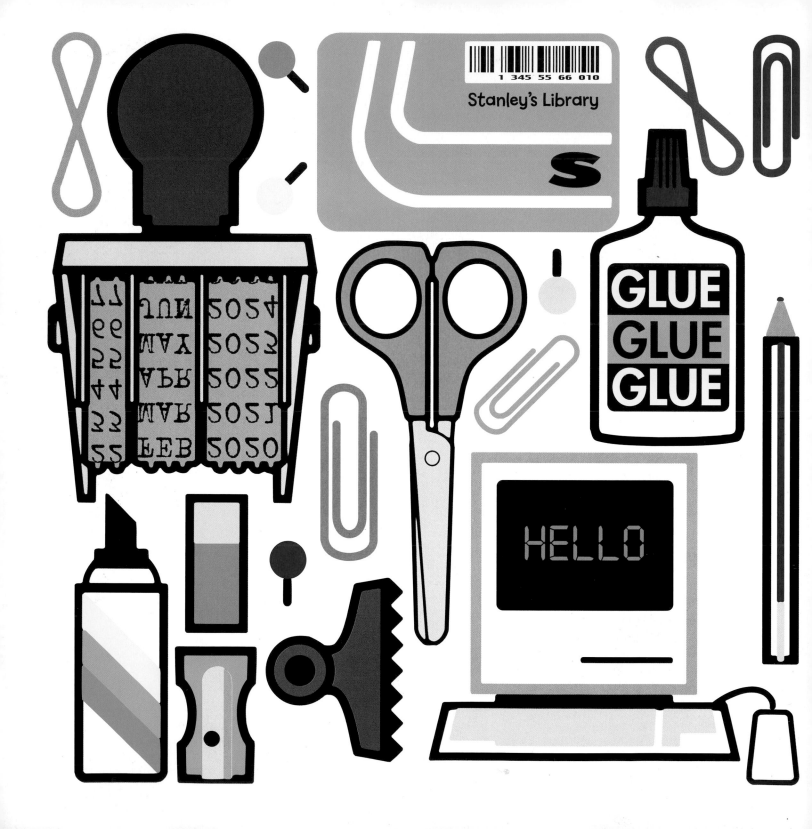

BOOK MARK

Stanley's Library
This book must be returned by the date below

22 FEB 2020

15 OCT 2020

-5 APR 2021

17 JAN 2022

11 DEC 2022

-2 MAR 2023

Free Ticket

Agatha Mouse reads from her book 'First Mouse in Space'

Stanley's Library **S**

Published by
PEACHTREE PUBLISHING COMPANY INC.
1700 Chattahoochee Avenue
Atlanta, Georgia 30318-2112
www.peachtree-online.com

Text and illustrations © 2021 by William Bee

First published in Great Britain in 2021 by Jonathan Cape, an imprint of Penguin Random House Children's
First United States version published in 2021 by Peachtree Publishing Company Inc.

The illustrations were rendered digitally.

Printed in March 2021 by Leo Paper in China
10 9 8 7 6 5 4 3 2 1 (hardcover)
10 9 8 7 6 5 4 3 2 1 (trade paperback)
First Edition

HC ISBN: 978-1-68263-313-7
PB ISBN: 978-1-68263-369-4

Cataloging-in-Publication Data is available from the Library of Congress.

Stanley's
Library

PEACHTREE
ATLANTA

It's going to be another busy day
at Stanley's Library.

Charlie tidies the bookshelves
while Stanley puts all sorts
of books onto his cart.

Next, he wheels the cart
into the library van.

Stanley drives to the park
and opens up the van's big doors.

The mobile library is ready for visitors!

First in line is Myrtle. She's returning
the five books all about cheese
she borrowed last week.

This week, she would like to borrow five MORE books—all about cheese, please!

Also at the park are Benjamin, Sophie, and Betty. Benjamin borrows a scary book.

Sophie borrows a scary, hairy book.
And Betty borrows a scary, hairy, fairy book!

Stanley spots Hattie oiling her motorbike.
He has a surprise for her that
he knows she will LOVE.

Thank you, Stanley!

Shamus chooses a book to help him with his rigging.

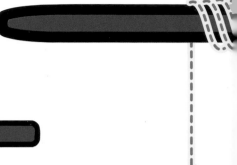

And Stanley has a book
for Little Woo, too.
Thank you, Stanley!

PIRATES!

LOTS OF KNOTS

LATEST EDITION

Stanley gets back to the library in time
to help Charlie arrange all the chairs . . .

. . . for a special event!

Everyone has dressed in space costumes.
Well, almost everyone . . .

They all settle down to hear
Agatha Mouse read from her new book.
Thank you, Agatha!

Well! What a busy day!

Stanley's
House

Time for supper!
Time for a bath!

And time for bed!
Goodnight, Stanley.

Stanley

If you liked **Stanley's Library** then you'll love these other books about Stanley:

Stanley the Builder
HC: $14.99 / 978-1-56145-801-1

Stanley's Garage
HC: $14.95 / 978-1-56145-804-2

Stanley the Farmer
HC: $14.95 / 978-1-56145-803-5

Stanley's School
HC: $14.99 / 978-1-68263-070-9

Stanley the Mailman
HC: $14.95 / 978-1-56145-867-7

Stanley's Store
HC: $14.95 / 978-1-56145-868-4

Stanley's Diner
HC: $14.99 / 978-1-56145-802-8

Stanley's Train
HC: $14.95 / 978-1-68263-108-9

Stanley's Fire Engine
HC: $14.99 / 978-1-68263-214-7

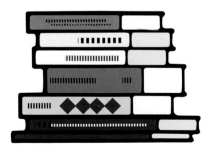

williambee